ASTERIX AND THE CHIEFTAIN'S SHIELD

TEXT BY GOSCINNY

DRAWINGS BY UDERZO

TRANSLATED BY ANTHEA BELL AND DEREK HOCKRIDGE

HODDER DARGAUD
LONDON SYDNEY AUCKLAND

ASTERIX IN OTHER COUNTRIES

Australia	Hodder Dargaud, Rydalmere Business Park, 10/16 South Street, Rydalmere, N.S.W. 2116, Australia
Austria	Delta Verlag, Postfach 1215, 7 Stuttgart 1, West Germany
Belgium	Dargaud Bénélux, 3 rue Kindermans, 1050 Brussels, Belgium
Brazil	Record Distribuidora, Rua Argentina 171, 20921 Rio de Janeiro, Brazil
Canada	Dargaud Canada, 307 Benjamin Hudon, St Laurent, Montreal H4N 1J1, Canada
Denmark	Serieforlaget A/S (Gutenberghus Group), Vognmagergade 11, 1148 Copenhagen K, Denmark
Esperanto	Delta Verlag, Postfach 1215, 7 Stuttgart 1, West Germany
Finland	Sanoma Corporation, P.O. Box 107, 00381 Helsinki 38, Finland
France	Dargaud Editeur, 12 Rue Blaise Pascal, 92201 Neuilly sur Seine, France *(titles up to and including Asterix in Belgium)* Les Editions Albert René, 26 Avenue Victor Hugo, 75116 Paris, France *titles from Asterix and the Great Divide, onwards)*
Germany, West	Delta Verlag, Postfach 1215, 7 Stuttgart 1, West Germany
Holland	Dargaud Bénélux, 3 rue Kindermans, 1050 Brussels, Belgium *(Distribution)* Van Ditmar b.v., Oostelijke Handelskade 11, 1019 BL, Amsterdam, Holland
Hong Kong	Hodder Dargaud, c/o United Publishers Book services, Stanhope House, 13th Floor, 734 King's Road, Hong Kong
Hungary	Nip Forum, Vojvode Misica 1-3, 2100 Novi Sad, Yugoslavia
India	*(Hindi)* Gowarsons Publishers Private Ltd, Gulab House, Mayapuri, New Delhi 110 064, India
Indonesia	Penerbit Sinar Harapan, J1. Dewi Sartika 136D, Jakarta Cawang, Indonesia
Israel	Dahlia Pelled Publishers, 5 Hamekoubalim St, Herzeliah 46447, Israel
Italy	Dargaud Italia, Via M. Buonarroti 38, 20145 Milan, Italy
Latin America	Grijalbo-Dargaud S.A., Deu y Mata 98-102, Barcelona 29, Spain
New Zealand	Hodder Dargaud, P.O. Box 3858, Auckland 1, New Zealand
Norway	A/S Hjemmet (Gutenburghus Group), Kristian den 4des gt 13, Oslo 1, Norway
Portugal	Meriberica, Avenida Alvares Cabral 84-1° Dto, 1296 Lisbon, Portugal
Roman Empire	*(Latin)* Delta Verlag, Postfach 1215, 7 Stuttgart 1, West Germany
Southern Africa	Hodder Dargaud, P.O. Box 548, Bergvlei, Sandton 2012, South Africa
Spain	Grijalbo-Dargaud S.A., Deu y Mata 98-102, Barcelona 29, Spain
Sweden	Hemmets Journal Forlag (Gutenberghus Group), Fack, 200 22 Malmö, Sweden
Switzerland	Interpress Dargaud S.A., En Budron B, 1052 Le Mont/Lausanne, Switzerland
Turkey	Kervan Kitabcilik, Basin Sanayii ve Ticaret AS, Tercuman Tesisleri, Topkapi-Istanbul, Turkey
USA	Dargaud Publishing International Ltd, 2 Lafayette Court, Greenwich, Conn. 06830, U.S.A.
Wales	*(Welsh)* Gwasg Y Dref Wen, 28 Church Road, Whitchurch, Cardiff, Wales
Yugoslavia	Nip Forum, Vojvode Misica 1-3, 2100 Novi Sad, Yugoslavia

Asterix and the Chieftain's Shield

ISBN 0 340 21394 9 (cased)
ISBN 0 340 22710 9 (limp)

Copyright © Dargaud Editeur 1968, Goscinny-Uderzo
English language text copyright © Hodder and Stoughton Ltd 1977

First published in Great Britain 1977 (cased)
This impression   91 92 93

First published in Great Britain 1978 (limp)
This impression   91 92 93

Published by Hodder Dargaud Ltd,
Mill Road, Dunton Green, Sevenoaks, Kent TN13 2YA

Printed in Belgium by Proost International Book Production

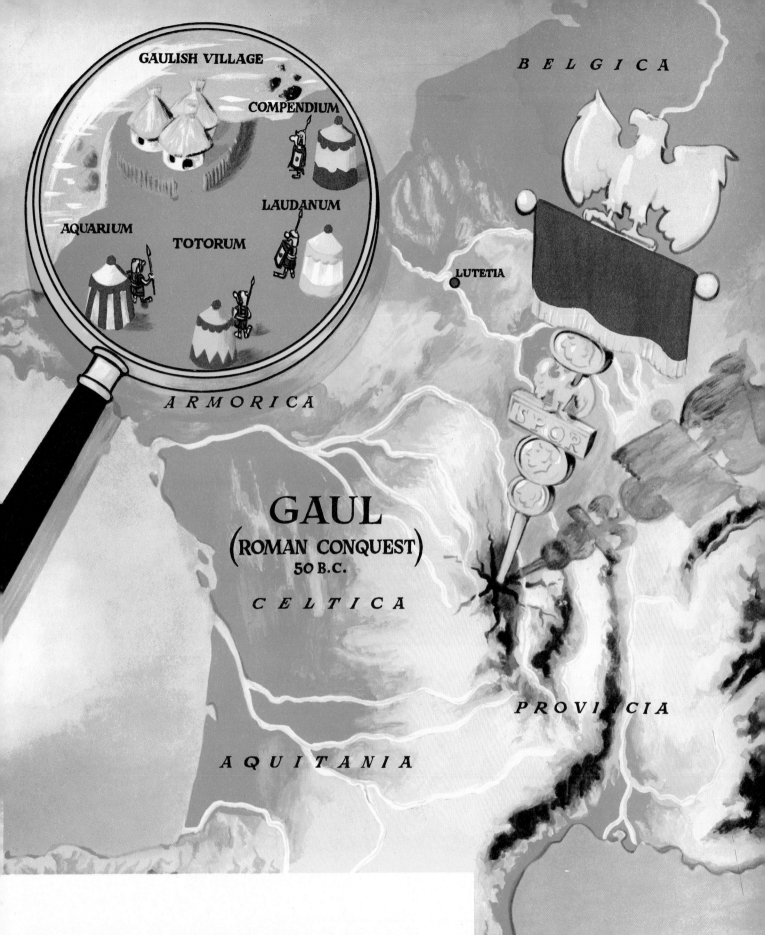

GAULISH VILLAGE

COMPENDIUM

LAUDANUM

AQUARIUM

TOTORUM

ARMORICA

BELGICA

LUTETIA

SPQR

GAUL
(ROMAN CONQUEST)
50 B.C.

CELTICA

AQUITANIA

PROVINCIA

The year is 50 BC. Gaul is entirely occupied by the Romans.
Well, not entirely… One small village of indomitable Gauls still
holds out against the invaders. And life is not easy for the
Roman legionaries who garrison the fortified camps of
Totorum, Aquarium, Laudanum and Compendium…

a few of the Gauls

Asterix, the hero of these adventures. A shrewd, cunning little warrior; all perilous missions are immediately entrusted to him. Asterix gets his superhuman strength from the magic potion brewed by the druid Getafix…

Obelix, Asterix's inseparable friend. A menhir delivery-man by trade; addicted to wild boar. Obelix is always ready to drop everything and go off on a new adventure with Asterix — so long as there's wild boar to eat, and plenty of fighting.

Getafix, the venerable village druid. Gathers mistletoe and brews magic potions. His speciality is the potion which gives the drinker superhuman strength. But Getafix also has other recipes up his sleeve…

Finally, Vitalstatistix, the chief of the tribe. Majestic, brave and hot-tempered, the old warrior is respected by his men and feared by his enemies. Vitalstatistix himself has only one fear; he is afraid the sky may fall on his head tomorrow. But as he always says, 'Tomorrow never comes.'

Cacofonix, the bard. Opinion is divided as to his musical gifts. Cacofonix thinks he's a genius. Everyone else thinks he's unspeakable. But so long as he doesn't speak, let alone sing, everybody likes him…

SO ALL GAUL IS OCCUPIED. ALL? NO! ONE LITTLE GAULISH VILLAGE IS STILL HOLDING OUT AGAINST THE INVADERS. A LITTLE VILLAGE WE KNOW VERY WELL, WHERE MORALE IS HIGH, AND ANY EXCUSE WILL DO TO HOLD A BANQUET WITH LOTS TO EAT AND DRINK. AS IT HAPPENS, THE LAST SUCH BANQUET HAS HAD SOME UNFORTUNATE CONSEQUENCES...

OOOOW! OOOOOOH! OH! OH! OH!

IS SOMEONE SLAUGHTERING A WILD BOAR?

NO, IT'S OUR BARD SINGING A LULLABY!

MAKE WAY FOR THE DRUID! CHIEF VITALSTATISTIX IS ILL!

IT'S THE SAME OLD STORY: THE DAY AFTER HE'S BEEN EATING AND DRINKING AND MAKING MERRY WITH THOSE BARBARIANS HE FEELS AS IF THE SKY HAD FALLEN ON HIS HEAD!

IT ISN'T MY HEAD THAT HURTS!

DOES IT HURT THERE, THEN?

AH, YES, HE'S GOT LIVER TROUBLE.

I NEVER KNEW ANYONE COULD GET LIVER TROUBLE...

OUUCH!

I WISH I WAS DEAD!

YOUR WIFE IMPEDIMENTA IS RIGHT, O CHIEF, I'M AFRAID YOU ATE AND DRANK RATHER TOO MUCH AT OUR LAST BANQUET.

I NEVER KNEW ANYONE COULD EAT TOO MUCH.

11

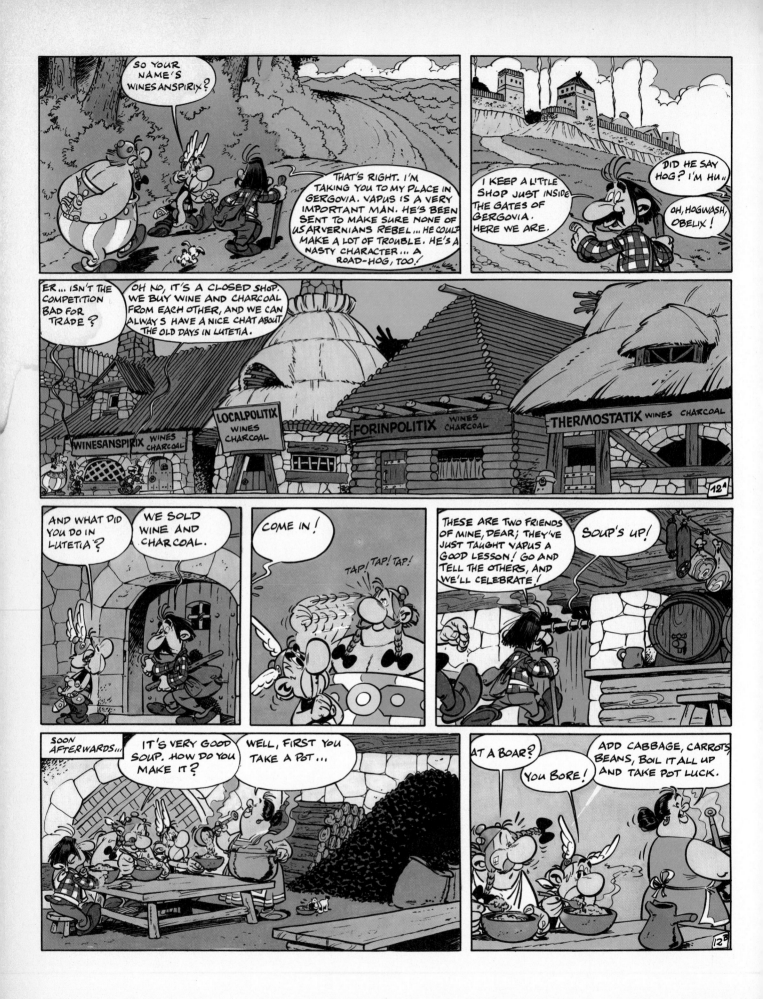

17

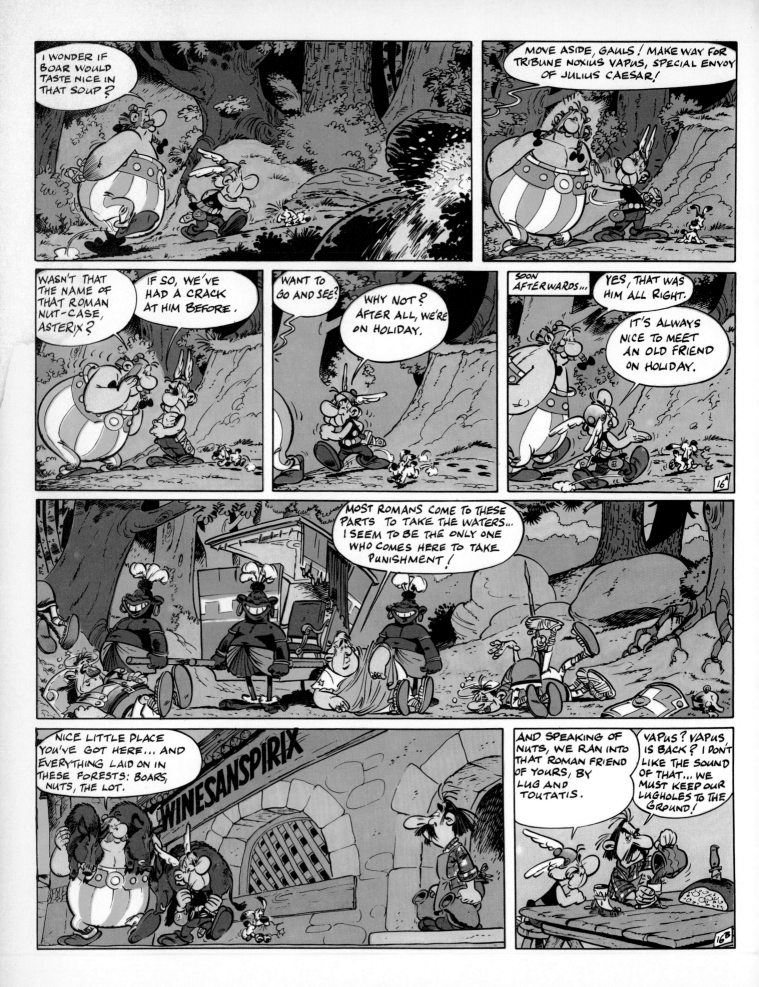

23

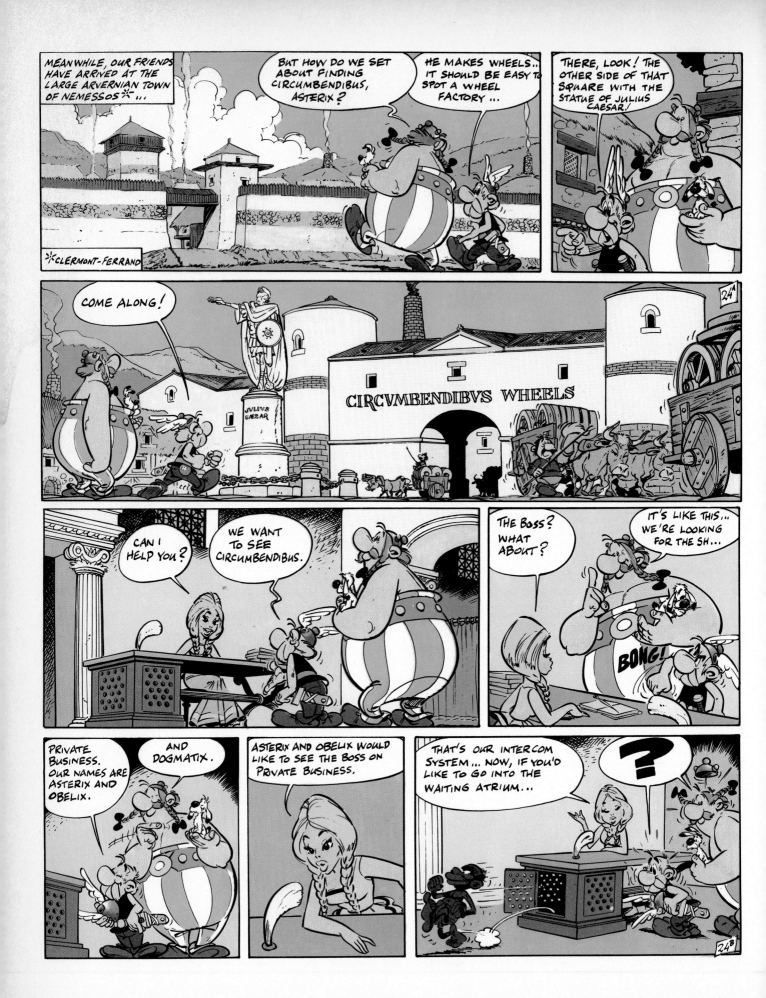

28

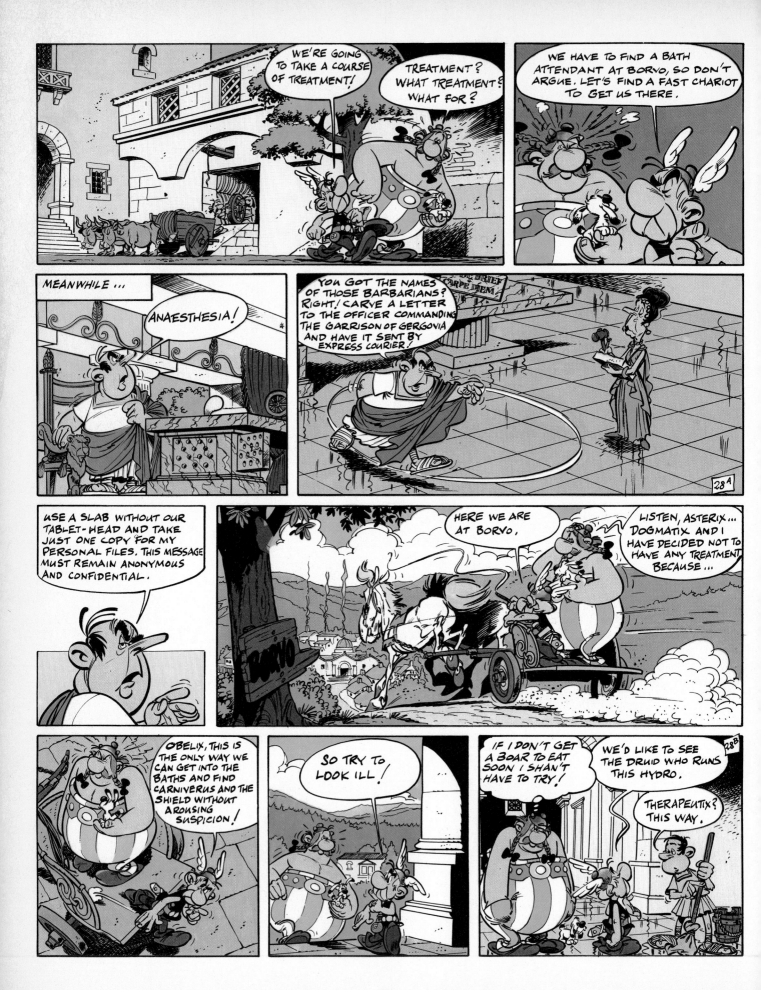

32

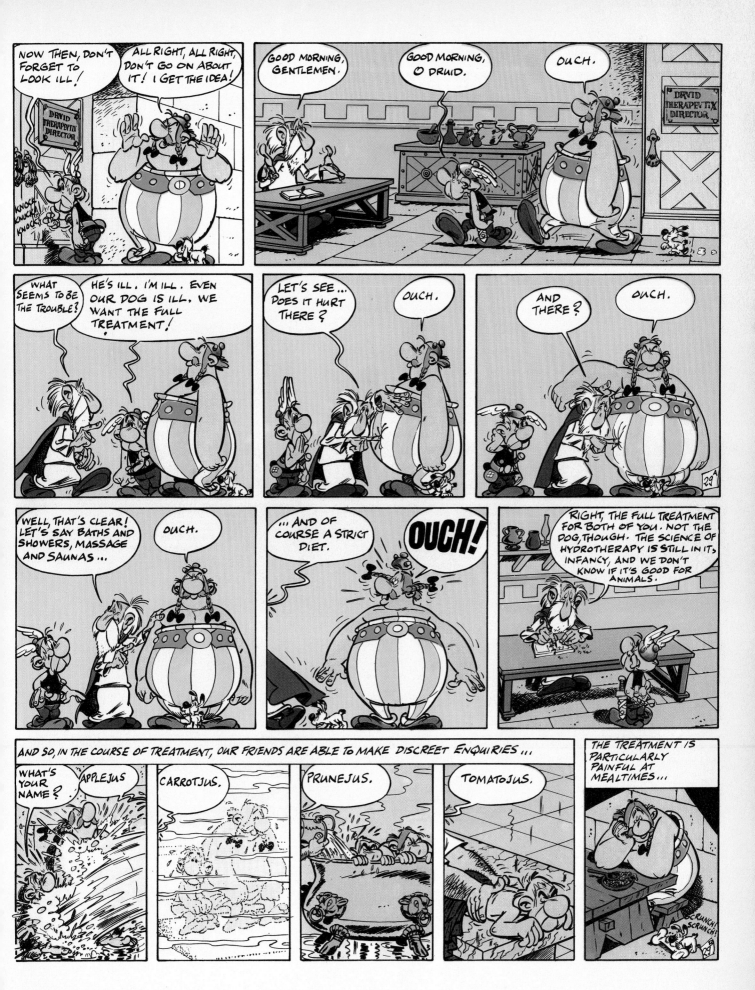

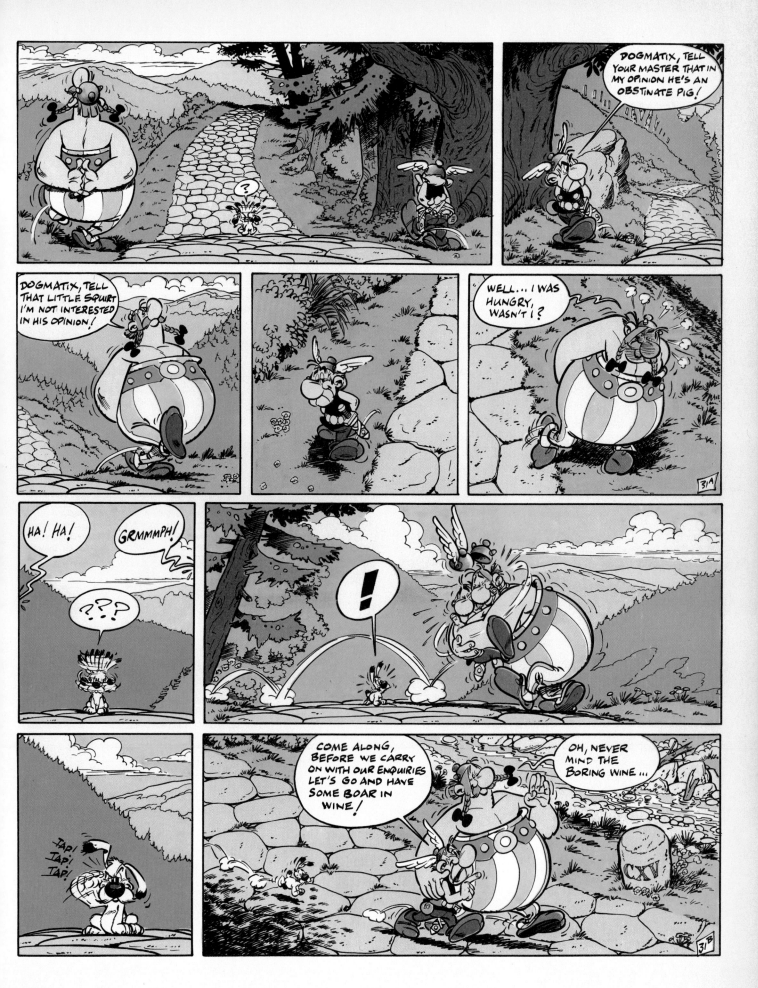

35

36

37

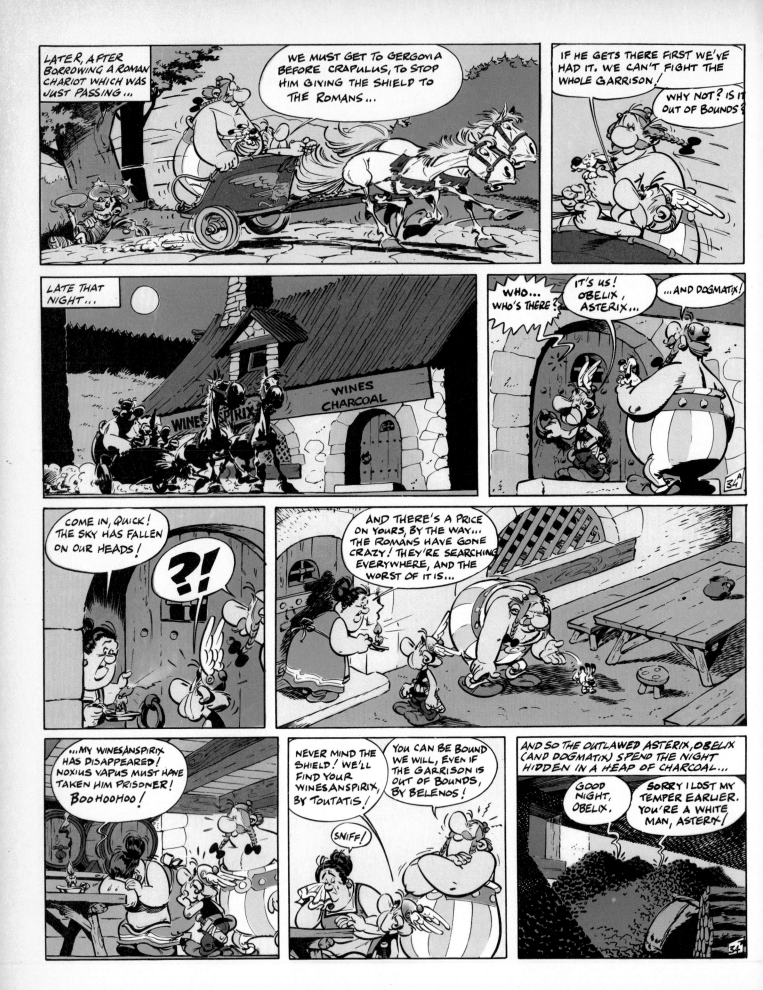

40

43

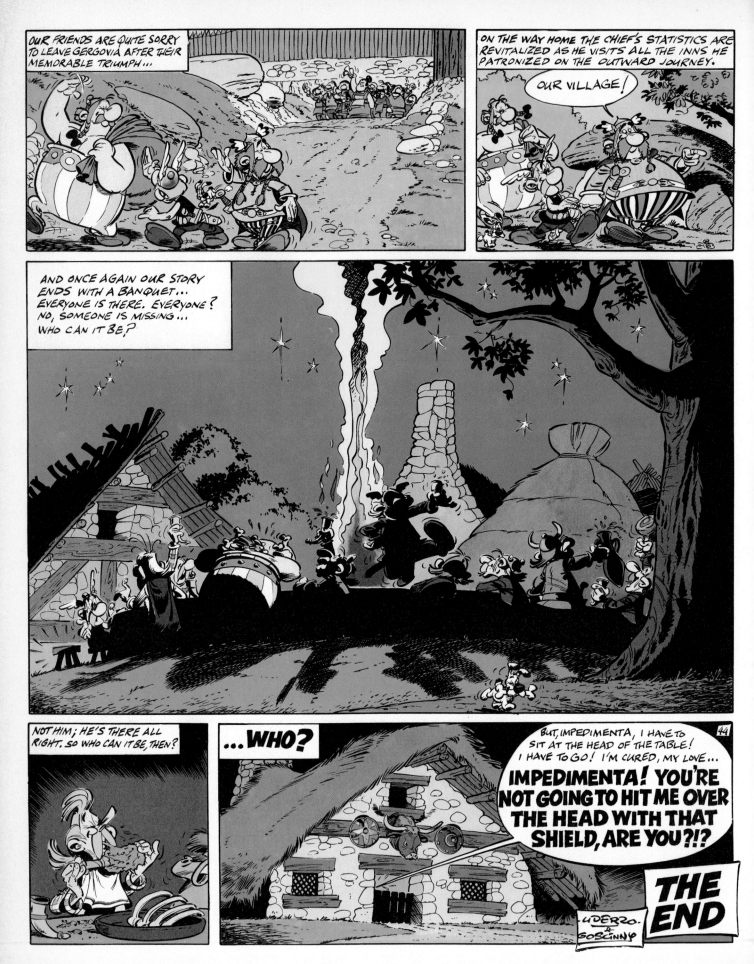

PRINTED IN BELGIUM BY
proost
INTERNATIONAL BOOK PRODUCTION